Park Stories: *Bushy Park*
& the Longford River

Park Stories: A Report to the Minister
© Will Self 2009

ISBN: 978-0-9558761-9-6

Series Editor: Rowan Routh

Published by The Royal Parks
www.royalparks.org.uk

Production by Strange Attractor Press
BM SAP, London, WC1N 3XX, UK
www.strangeattractor.co.uk

Cover design: Ali Hutchinson

Park Stories devised by Rowan Routh

The Royal Parks gratefully acknowledges the financial support of Arts
Council England.

Printed by Kennet Print, Devizes, UK on
100% post-consumer recycled Cyclus offset
paper using vegetable-based inks.

A Report to the Minister

Will Self

THE
ROYAL
PARKS

A Report to the Minister

Madam, I am not an especially poetic man – neither my
upbringing, nor my life experience has encouraged such
tendencies. Or am I deluding myself? At just past dawn on a
winter morning, each blade of grass spun from sugary frost,
swathed in the silken haze of low-angled rays lancing into
ground mist – then, between the pools and the plantations,
where the stag stands petrified – his very stasis a fierce
compression of all the fleet movements he's ever made
and ever will – then... well, despite all the routine tasks, the
paperwork, the management of the ground contractors, the
liaison with community groups, yes, I concede, I do open
myself to the inspiration of this place, feel it swell inside my
chest, then billow from me, even as the breath billows from
the nostrils of the stag, to condense – so thick and white as
to be almost tangible – then disperse.

    ·   Be that as it may, I have never – I repeat *never* –
given in to this feeling to the point where I've forgotten my
statutory obligations or failed to conform to best practice.
In the matter of this child, whose existence and manner
of life have come to the attention of Constable Harris, I
can assure you that my conscience is clear: I have neither
compromised my own professionalism, nor that of my staff;
I have not lain the Royal Parks open to any public censure
or media scrutiny, and I doubt very much the possibility of a
successful prosecution under the Health and Safety at Work
Act (1974).

      I've been told that there's a roost of some 6,500
ring-necked parakeets in the strip of woodland alongside
Esher rugby ground. I confess, I've never actually been
there to observe them – my duties keep me here, and here I

live – yet it must be an astonishing sight. I picture them in a long row of poplars, their myriad green-gold and iridescent wings flickering between the boughs and twigs – which at this season are a child's scribble of black lines. What I'm trying to say is... that we have more than our fair share of ring-necks, here in the park they scrap in the trees and dip between them; to my ear they make an alien racket. I'm no ornithologist, and would've assumed that they were ousting native species from their own niches – perhaps severely affecting biodiversity. However, I'm assured that this isn't the case.

I'm searching for... an analogy here: the ring-necks; the American GIs stationed here during the Second War; before them, in the Depression, there was a camp here for starveling kids from the East End; and before them, in the First War, there were the Royal Canadians. Green-gold, green, grey and buff – odd alien birds all. Still, the park has managed to accommodate them all – nurture them all. Constable Harris is a conscientious policeman – no one doubts that, yet he lacks... how can I put it, a certain fluidity of thought. The park is a primordial heath land, part tamed, its wild grasses and furze corralled into open glades, its trees drilled into straight avenues, or else enclosed in plantations. Most importantly, there is the water: the ponds, the rills and the streams. The Longford River – dug in the seventeenth century at the behest of Charles the First – is well known; it runs through the western side of the park on its way to Hampton Court Palace. Few suspect that this ancient water supply is complemented by a modern one: the three-metre bore culvert, buried forty more beneath the park, that links the Thames with the metropolis's mighty ring main. Moreover, the park occupies a tongue of land, edged on three sides by the saliva flow of the river, while to the west, the vast reservoirs – Island Barn, Queen Elizabeth II – reflect in their rippling mirrors the odd titanium fish that surface on to the runways of Heathrow. Is it too fanciful to suggest that it's these waters – whether limpid, pulsing, or coursing – that create the ebb and flow of our imaginations? Those of us, that is, who have spent long enough in the park.

Constable Harris, dutifully patrolling the Lime Avenue, then glancing back from time to time at the Diana Fountain – what might he, a stranger, think? I do not mean to be... patronising, but on the basis of his subsequent behaviour, I cannot believe him to be well versed in mythology. I ask you, Minister, on that cold and bright and misty morning, when the pool in which the statue seemed to float was a circlet of molten silver where melted, and one of iron-grey where not... and the scraps of waterfowl tore themselves from the dank sheet of the sky, who, knowing the myth of Arethusa – how she was relentlessly pursued by Apheus, the river god, until their waters wantonly mingled – who could prevent themselves from cascading through dream grottos, or tumbling down fanciful cataracts?

Not Constable Harris. He saw a boy clad in leggings of waxed khaki cloth, bare-chested but with a cloak of the same. He judged the child to be about eleven years of age, and noted that he was armed – a bow slung over one shoulder and quiver over the other. That the bow had been expertly carved from a yew bough, while the quiver had been improvised using a tennis racket holder – the logo 'Wilson' was still clearly visible – should have alerted Harris to the fact that this was no ordinary boy, just as the leap of a steel-tipped and nylon-fletched arrow to the bowstring might've convinced a less prosaic fellow that he was in the presence of a young Actaeon, who, pursued by his own hounds – a motley pack, Harris reported, that included dachshunds, staffies and a labradoodle – was fleeing from the fatal transgression of witnessing a goddess, naked, at her toilet.

Why not? The park's landscaping would serve well enough for the background of a Titian, what with its groves, its pools, its ivy-choked tree stumps and masonry lumps. The boy stood transfixed for long moments, his bow half-drawn – a small stag at bay, then he turned, dashed over the brick bridge, and entered the Woodland Garden by diving headlong between the steel strands of the fence while his dogs snapped at his heels. Harris, not equipped for an instant to doubt the reality of what he had seen, clung – as the literal-minded so often do – to the very letter of the law: no sporting activities are permitted except in designated areas of the park, while in order to preserve biodiversity, dogs are prohibited in the Woodland Garden. So, he set off in pursuit, his heavy boots crunching over the frosted turf.

By means of casual chats over cups of tea in the park office – perhaps with me, or with other members of my staff; or there might've been small asides made as Harris patrolled with his more experienced colleagues in the Safer Park Team. Then again, being a conscientious – if by-the-book policeman – Harris would, in the course of time, have talked both to the officially designated Friends of the Park, and also with the regulars. In this connection one thinks, immediately, of the man in the three-wheeled chair, whose dogs pull him each day, at speed, along the path beside the Royal Paddocks, from Hampton Court Gate to Church Grove Gate; or of the solitary lady of a certain age, who feeds white bread sandwiches – carefully shorn of their crusts – to the ducks on the Leg-of-Mutton pond. Any of us would've been in a position to gently educate him – at first only with hints, later by analogy, until finally, having proved himself... receptive, he was given concrete information.

When I have the responsibility of interviewing prospective staff I'm able to look them in the eye. I may be questioning them about coppicing, shift rotation or expanding the visitor centre, but I'm not listening to their replies – only checking for a certain waywardness, a way of looking not *at* me, but through my eyes, as if they were windows into another world. These are the men and women that I hire, confident that while they may perform their duties perfectly adequately – locking and unlocking the vehicular gates, checking fishing permits, stopping cars from parking on the verges – they will be only too happy to dive headlong into that other world as soon as the opportunity is presented. Unfortunately, I have no such jurisdiction over the Safer Park Team.

In the Woodland Garden – really the old arboretum of Bushy House, gone feral over the centuries – Harris saw what? I can envision it, for I've seen it too, usually at dawn or dusk – or on the night of the full moon, when, seeing that I'm alone they've chosen to reveal themselves. Or else, I've surprised them: gathering fungi, netting fish, or quartering a deer. Then, they've remained squatting on their haunches, digging sticks or knives in their heads, their wild eyes on me, each one like that emblematic stag, caught in perfect equilibrium between fight and flight. That their raiment is a bizarre confusion between the 21st century and the upper Palaeolithic – Gore-Tex leggings, waxed cotton cloaks, kapok-padded penis sheaths – is less remarkable than the collision in their expressions between the wistfulness of dog-walkers and the wariness of those who hunt with dogs.

On this particular frosty morning, the hunting party – for that is who they were – took too long to assess the threat that Harris presented. When they fled – snatching up the carcasses of the rabbits they were skinning – they left behind two small piles of steaming entrails and the boy but lately come, who the policeman had advanced upon – then grabbed. The dogs – trained to be silent – vanished among the trees with the others, while the boy fought like a cornered vixen protecting her earth. Unfortunately his bites and scratches only stiffened Harris's resolve, and so I was woken – from uneasy dreams: a crystal palace burning, ladies in full skirts and gentlemen in frock coats dancing a stately pavane in a spreading pool of molten glass, their animal masks blackened by the smoke – to discover the irate officer, who was banging on the door of my lodging, while his captive span and spat.

The matter of the deer will, I know, be of concern to those unfamiliar with open-access land management and best practice when it comes to sustainability. Historically the herd has maintained its population, with approximately 300 animals, half roe and half fallow deer. This is the summer headcount after calving in late May. The cull of the males takes place in late September, that of the females in November. Obviously, given the public's tendency to sentimentalise, the cull is not something we widely advertise: we put signs up that restrict public access in no uncertain terms, while remaining discrete about the reasons for this restriction. That we are able to rely on stealthy and accurate bowmen for a proportion of the necessary kills is a great asset. They also butcher the carcasses and make use of everything: meat, fat, skin and antlers – even the animals' sinews, which they dry for use as bowstrings. Even the fluffiest of environmentalists would surely approve.

The same could be said of our fisheries management. Some of those who pay for course fishing licences would be put out to discover that while they're required to throw their catch back, others are keeping it. But only some – the rest know, and do not begrudge the loss of the tench, the bream and the pike, understanding that these are a valuable source of protein for a traditional people. These anglers also know that those who take the fish also keep the ponds free of duckweed and blue-green algae – that they manage the resource for everyone.

I did try to persuade Constable Harris to release his captive – and this was undoubtedly a mistake. I couldn't help myself, the boy, like any creature accustomed to range freely was terrified by being deprived of his liberty, and of course, as a native of the park he knew nothing of the wider world, and had no conception of having done anything wrong. Yes, I urged Harris not to take the child to the police station, and panicking, told him not to forget what he'd seen. Believe me, Minister, it wasn't my own position that motivated me. I couldn't care if the Department suspends me, so long as I remain free to wander the park in all seasons, to see the hooded crows cluster on the hollow trunks of long-dead elms, to watch the fritillaries bob across the wildflower meadow, to gaze upon the massy candelabras of the flowering chestnuts... The thought of that young and noble savage, confined to a 'care' unit, forced into constricting clothing, then fed processed pap instead of good vegetables and fresh-killed meat, all the time keening for his people and his dogs – it's this that cuts me to the quick.

What now, Minister? What will be done now that Harris's report has done the rounds? This human culture has lasted, maintaining a delicate balance with its environment, for many decades – possibly centuries. It was like this when I was appointed chief keeper; my predecessor told me it was the same when he came to the park, and that the chief keeper he succeeded related that he himself had only maintained a pre-existing status quo. How can we explain the endurance of such a singular... phenomenon? The park may be large but it is surrounded on all sides by a mighty conurbation. Be that as it may, West London is not a brick wilderness, it has its own culture and folkways; early on in my time here I realised that between those of the park, and those that visit it there was a deep and enduring tolerance.

So what if the occasional cabbage or handful of runner beans is taken from the allotments bordering the park, the people who tend them know they go to sustain a proud and free people, a people who play a crucial role in promoting social cohesion and community values. To give you but one example, Minister: in recent years teenage gangs

took to using the park for binge drinking and drug-taking.
Their parties were unruly – they set fires and left mounds
of litter, some of them became dangerously intoxicated.
This might've grown into a serious problem were it not for
the intercession of older and wilder people. They took the
ringleaders away and in suitably ritualised settings – a full
moon, a still pool and a masked shaman – employed certain
herbs and fungi to inculcate in these wayward youths a
proper respect for the derangement of the senses. Oh! That
wild derangement – that can draw a person closer and closer
to the gods, so close that their beauty maddens... their divine
musk stings... your eyes!

    Not that budgetary matters should ever be
neglected, Minister, I understand that as well as any other
Royal Parks employee. However, just as there's been
no major crime in the park reported for years, so our
cost control has been consistent – in some years we've
significantly under-spent. This wouldn't have been possible
without these... others, who help my staff to harvest the
freshwater mussels from the streams and culverts. Few casual
visitors to the park understand how crucial such symbiotic
relationships are to its effective management. I've lost count
of the number of times I've been asked why it is that all the
tree foliage is so neatly cropped – each massy crown levelled
off sharply at its base. But just as the deer maintain this
perfect browse line, so the resident human population keeps
the park neat and tidy in a myriad unseen ways: clearing the
brush, spiriting off fallen boughs, removing the rubbish.

    So, no major crimes for years and hardly any minor
ones, while visitor numbers have risen year-on-year; a highly
successful outreach programme to local schools, while the
fabric of the park has been maintained rigorously within
budget – surely Minister, given these indisputable facts,
it would hardly be in anyone's interest to have the park...
cleared of its... indigenous human population? These are a

wily and resourceful folk, deeply versed in bush craft. Given the size of the park it would take thousands rather than hundreds of personnel – police would be insufficient; the army would have to be called out. The media would – I'm sure you'll agree – have a field day.

Then there are the locals – the park's principle users. Don't make the mistake, Minister, of imagining that these ordinary-seeming suburbanites are merely passive; the relationship between the residents of Molesey, Hampton, Teddington, Kingston and those who we call 'the Bushy', is a complex and ever-evolving symbiosis. For, while there is only a core population of some 200 Bushy, this fluctuates both seasonally and at weekends. A middle class dog walker, uniformed in a padded gilet, jeans and a headscarf – her golden retriever flushes a rabbit that crazily leaps and bounds across the tussocks. In a series of fluid movements she divests herself of her clothing, snatches up a slim spear that's planted, ready, in a thicket. Then, joined by a party of others – who, like her, are as bare and brown as Nereids – she goes to the hunt!

A lab assistant quits the grounds of the National Physical Laboratory on the north side of the park. He's ground down by a long morning developing the most accurate measurement standards conceivable of. He carries, perhaps, a ham sandwich and a can of coke – is intent on a bench from where he can see a corner of the sky, hear birdsong, smell grass. Five, ten – or is it a hundred minutes later, for he has lost all track of time – he splashes through the shallows of the Longford River. His naked toes seek out the nacreous shells of mussels while he laughs and jokes with his boon companions.

Retired bank employees, bored housewives, troubled adolescents – all manner of folk find sanctuary with the Bushy, some for an hour, others a month. Many return again and again over the years. The Friends of Bushy

Park, Minister, are not a regulation little group of amateur functionaries, but an extensive and dispersed tribe of part-time hunter-gatherers. Were you to mobilise the forces of the law against them, you might find yourself responsible for West London's Little Big Horn.

Of course, I don't mean to denigrate those visitors from further a field who are unaware of the park's ulterior life – they have their place: driving in from the Teddington Gate to admire Wren's stately chestnut avenue, stopping at the car park for a tea, a pee and a short stroll. To those of us who are here year-round, they appear far more exotic than any ring-neck parakeet, flocking in their iridescent nylon jackets, then mounting their steely chariots and riding away. Surely, Minister, while giving due consideration to these visitors'... amenities, the Department also has a statutory obligation to protect those... others, whose entire being remains fused with this place, with its dells and glades and rills; those who, as the horned moon lifts from the shoulder of Hampton Hill, link arms to dance around the Diana Fountain, while in the distance the last train leaves Hampton Court station and accelerates, clickety-clack, towards the inner city.

As I stated at the beginning of this report, I am not, Minister, a poet; yet surely you do not need a poet to convey to you quite how cruelly dull, how bureaucratically null, how practically useless are the words of Constable Harris. Or am I – as the antlers plunge from my forehead and I fall forward on to my front hooves, and my breath billows from my nostrils, and I tremble with all the compacted urgency of the chase – deluding myself?